W9-CME-715

The Brothers Grimm

RAPUNZEL

retold by Amy Ehrlich

pictures by Kris Waldherr

DIAL BOOKS FOR YOUNG READERS
New York

For my grandmother
K.W.

Published by Dial Books for Young Readers
A Division of Penguin Books USA Inc.
2 Park Avenue New York, New York 10016

Published simultaneously in Canada
by Fitzhenry & Whiteside Limited, Toronto
Pictures copyright © 1989 by Kris Waldherr
Text used by permission of Random House, Inc.
Text copyright © 1989 by Amy Ehrlich
All rights reserved
Typography by Amelia Lau Carling
Printed in Hong Kong by
South China Printing Company (1988) Limited
First Edition
E
1 3 5 7 9 10 8 6 4 2

Library of Congress Cataloging in Publication Data
Ehrlich, Amy, 1942—   Rapunzel /
retold by Amy Ehrlich: illustrated by Kris Waldherr.
p.   cm.
Summary: A beautiful girl with extraordinarily long
golden hair is imprisoned in a lonely tower by a witch.
ISBN 0-8037-0654-5.   ISBN 0-8037-0655-3 (lib. bdg.)
[1. Fairy tales. 2. Folklore—Germany.]
I. Waldherr, Kris, ill. II. Rapunzel. III. Title.
PZ8.E32Rap 1989   [E]—dc19   88-25918   CIP   AC

The full-color artwork was prepared using pencil,
colored pencils, and watercolors. Pastels were also used
on the scenic borders. The paintings were color-separated
and reproduced in red, blue, yellow, and black halftones.

A man and his wife had long wished for a child, and after many years had passed it seemed that at last they were to have one. Their house was in the countryside and at the back was a little window that overlooked a beautiful garden planted with vegetables and flowers. But it was surrounded by a high wall and no one dared go in there, for it belonged to a powerful witch.

One day the wife was standing by the window and looking down into the garden when she saw a bed of rapunzel greens. They looked so fresh and lovely that she longed for some to eat. Each day her longing increased until she became pale and sickly and would take no other food. Then her husband was alarmed and said, "What is the matter, dear wife?"

"Ah," she answered, "if I cannot have some of the rapunzel from the garden behind our house, I shall surely die."

Her husband, who loved her, knew he would have to bring her the rapunzel she wanted, no matter what the cost. At twilight he climbed over the wall into the witch's garden. Quickly he picked a handful of the rapunzel and took it to his wife. She made a salad and ate it greedily, but she was still not satisfied. The taste was so wonderful that she had to have more of the rapunzel at once. She wept and begged until her husband agreed to go back into the witch's garden.

Again in the twilight he set out, but this time when he climbed over the wall, he saw the witch standing before him.

"How dare you come into my garden and steal my rapunzel!" she said angrily. "You will have to suffer for it."

The man was terribly afraid. "Please take pity on me," he answered. "I had to come here. My wife saw the rapunzel from the window and her longing for it is so great that she will die if she cannot have some."

Then the rage left the witch's face and she said, "If what you say is true, I shall allow you to take away as much as you want —but on one condition. You must give me the child your wife is carrying. I will bring it up as my own and care for it like a mother."

In his fear the man consented to everything, and when the baby was born, the witch came for her and gave her the name Rapunzel.

As the years went by, Rapunzel grew to be the most beautiful child imaginable. When she was twelve, the witch took her away and shut her up in a tower that stood in a forest.

It had no doors and only a little window high in the wall.
Each time the witch wanted to come in, she would stand below
it and cry:

Rapunzel, Rapunzel,
Let down your hair.

Rapunzel had magnificent long hair, as fine as spun gold. When she heard the witch's voice, she would unfasten her braids and twist them around a hook by the window. Then the hair would fall twenty feet down and the witch would climb up the wall on it.

Some time later it happened that the king's son was riding through the forest and passed close by the tower. As he did, he heard a song so lovely and clear that he stood still to listen. Rapunzel sang each day in her loneliness and it was her voice that he heard.

The king's son wanted to climb up to her and looked for a door to the tower, but none was to be found.

He rode home, but his thoughts were haunted by Rapunzel's sweet song, and he returned again and again to the forest to listen to it.

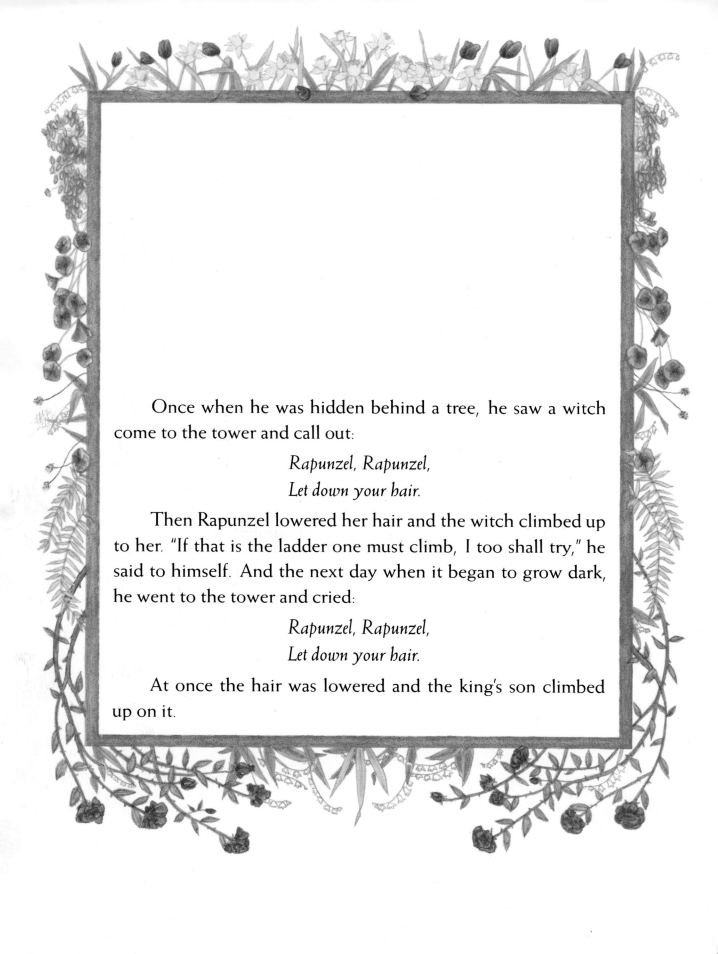

Once when he was hidden behind a tree, he saw a witch come to the tower and call out:

> *Rapunzel, Rapunzel,*
> *Let down your hair.*

Then Rapunzel lowered her hair and the witch climbed up to her. "If that is the ladder one must climb, I too shall try," he said to himself. And the next day when it began to grow dark, he went to the tower and cried:

> *Rapunzel, Rapunzel,*
> *Let down your hair.*

At once the hair was lowered and the king's son climbed up on it.

Rapunzel was terrified, for she had never seen a man, but the king's son spoke to her gently and told her how beautiful her song had been. Then she lost her fear, and when he asked if she would have him for her husband, she agreed. She could see that he was young and handsome, and she thought that he was kind. "He will love me better than old Mother Gothel does," she said to herself, and she laid her hand in his.

"I will gladly go with you," she told him. "But I do not know how I am to get down from this tower. I'll tell you what. When you come each evening, you must bring me a skein of silk to twist into a ladder. As soon as it is long enough, I will come down upon it and we will ride away on your horse."

The witch knew nothing until one day Rapunzel said to her, "Tell me, Mother Gothel, why is it you are so much heavier to draw up than the young prince?"

"Oh, you wicked child!" cried the witch. "I thought I had separated you from all the world and yet you have deceived me." In her rage she seized Rapunzel's beautiful hair, twisted it twice round her left hand, and cut it off with a pair of shears.

When the hair lay upon the ground, she took Rapunzel into a vast wilderness and abandoned her there.

In the evening the witch returned to the tower and tied the
hair to a hook by the window. She waited until the prince called:

> Rapunzel, Rapunzel,
> Let down your hair.

And then she quickly lowered it.

As soon as the prince climbed up, he saw the witch.

"Ah," she cried mockingly, "you've come to fetch your love. But the pretty bird has flown. Never shall you see her again."

In his pain and grief the prince leaped from the tower, and though he was not killed, his eyes were pierced by the thorns among which he fell. Weeping and lamenting he roamed about blindly in the forest and had nothing but roots and berries to eat.

After many years of wandering alone he at last came into the wilderness where Rapunzel had been living in poverty and wretchedness.

The prince heard a clear, sweet voice and it seemed so familiar to him that he went toward it. Rapunzel knew him at once and fell weeping upon his neck. Two of her tears wetted his eyes and they grew clear again so he could see all that was before him.

Then he took Rapunzel back to his kingdom, where they were greeted with great rejoicing, and they lived for a long time afterward in happiness and peace.

Kris Waldherr

was born in New Jersey and received her Bachelor of Fine Arts degree from the School of Visual Arts in New York. She worked on the paintings for this, her first book, while living in an old cottage on the moors of Devon, England. She now lives in New York City.

Amy Ehrlich

has retold a series of classic fairy tales illustrated for Dial by Susan Jeffers, including *Thumbelina*, *The Wild Swans*, *The Snow Queen*, and *Cinderella*. She is the author of such original picture books and Dial Easy-to-Read Books as *Zeek Silver Moon; Leo, Zack, and Emmie;* and *Leo, Zack, and Emmie Together Again;* as well as a novel, *Where It Stops, Nobody Knows*. Ms. Ehrlich was a children's book editor at a major New York house before she moved to Vermont, where she lives with her husband and son.

*Portrayed above is the rapunzel, more commonly known as rampion,
a flowering plant grown in much of Europe, North Africa, and western Asia.
The roots and leaves are used as salad greens.*